Homework:

Write about an interesting animal from our field trip to the aquarium.

For my husband, Matthew,
who inspires me daily.

And for my son, Fletcher,
who lives for silliness.

—CF

Anatomy of a Seahorse

pectoral fin

coronet

eye

sn

anal fin

brood pouch
(males only)

Dylan McLeod

This Is a → Seahorse

By. Cassandra Federman

Mr. Tucker's class

10, 20

Albert Whitman & Company
Chicago, Illinois

This Is a ➡ Seahorse

By: Cassandr...

Good day!
I'm quite majestic,
am I not?

Mr....

October 1...20

huge nose

big belly

tail

tail

At first I thought seahorses were like land horses, but you can't ride a seahorse.

Ride a seahorse? Pffff...preposterous idea.

Because seahorses are too tiny, and they're the SLOWEST fish in the world.

Surely not the *slowest*.

Those fish haven't moved a fin since my arrival.

Seahorses are actually more like other non-horse animals.

They can
grip things
with their tails,
like opossums.

Those nasty creatures?
You won't catch me holding
tails with one of them.

Seahorses have long snouts, like anteaters do, to help them eat.

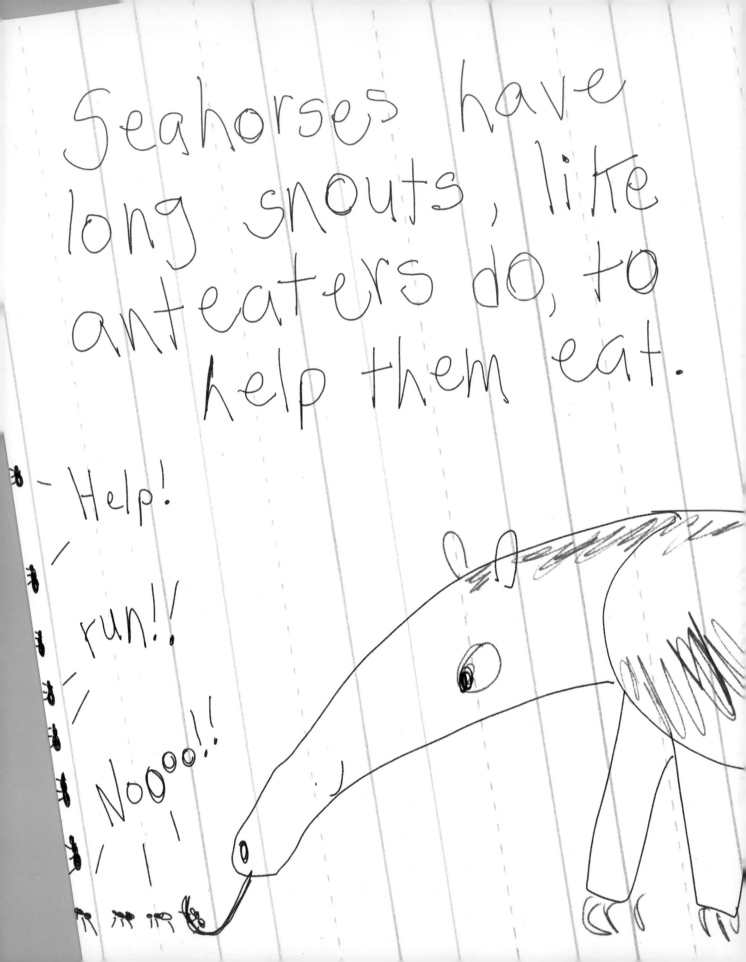

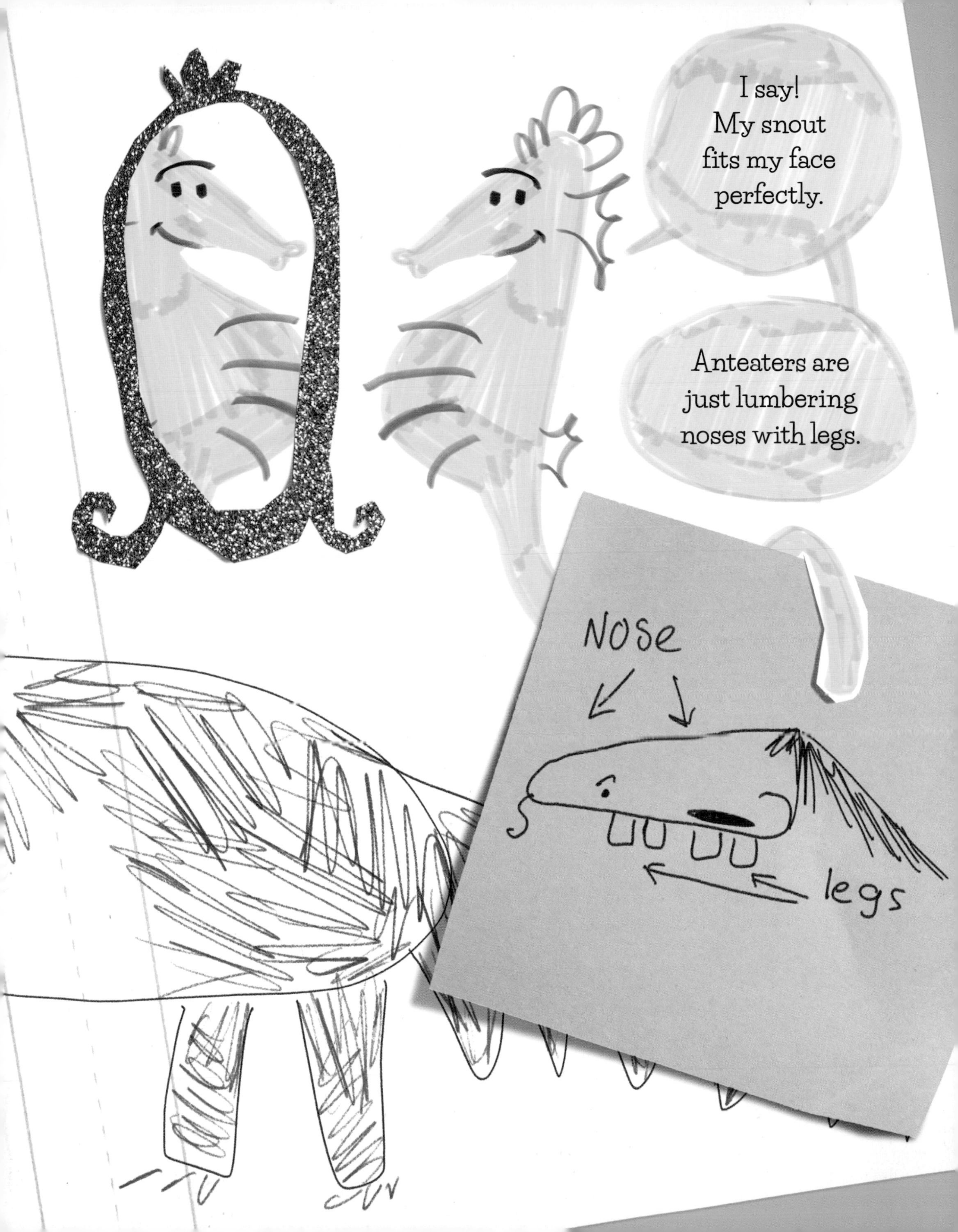

I say! My snout fits my face perfectly.
Anteaters are just lumbering noses with legs.
NOSE
legs

They dance for their mates the way blue-footed booby birds do.

Correction:
I dance WITH my mate. Each and every morning!

Seahorses can camouflage themselves, like octopuses do.

EGAD!
Octopuses are hideous, eight-armed SEA MONSTERS, whilst I am a handsome no-armed seahorse.
WE COULDN'T BE...

MORE

DIFFERENT!

A really long time ago, Greek people called seahorses "hippocamps", which means

HIPPOCAMPS

"HORSE SEA MONSTERS."

You know who *is* a monster? YOU!

Seahorses growl when they get angry. Like dogs.

I'll not dignify that with a response.

I wonder if seahorses also...

smell butts?!

GRRROWL!
I would never!

SNAP

Enough nonsense.
None of these other animals
are nearly as charming and
unique as seahorses.

There is one thing about **DADDY** seahorses, though, that is **NOT** like any other animal.

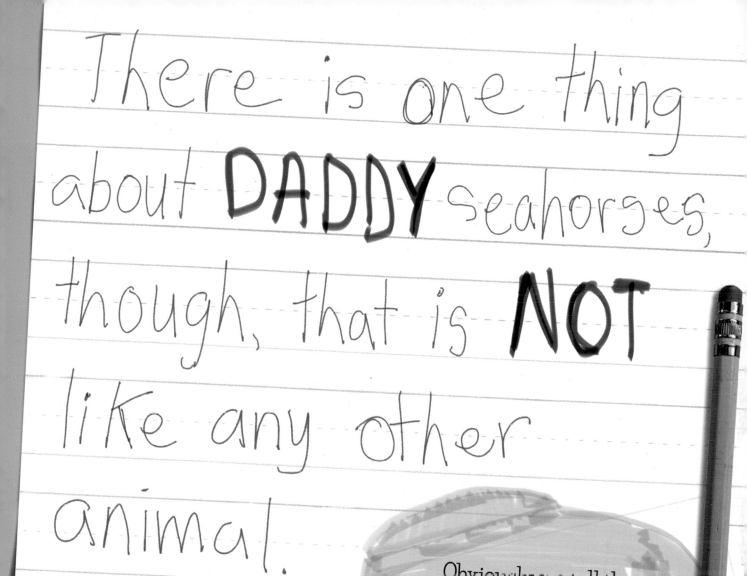

Obviously we tell the BEST jokes. Why did the seahorse cross the road? He didn't! There are no roads in the ocean, silly. Ha! Classic.

GIVE BIRTH!

I used to love seahorses because I thought they were just like land horses.

Harper

Alanna

Madelyn

WAIT!

Used to love?

But now I think seahorses are super **WEIRD!**

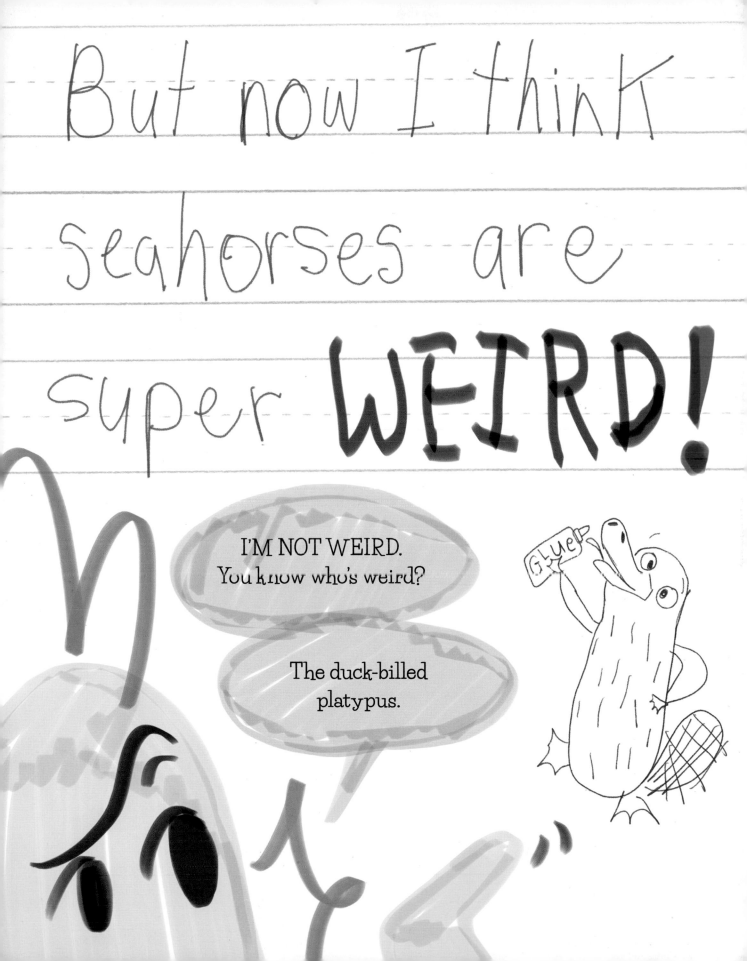

I'M NOT WEIRD.
You know who's weird?

The duck-billed platypus.

AND BEING WEIRD IS COOL.

Oh.

Hmmm. I never thought of it that way. You may very well be right!

But the water bear is even WEIRDER!!!

Called me a monster!

Called me weird!

GRRR!

Er, I may have been a tad hasty just now.

Called me a...um... ninnypoop?

Have you all heard the news that being weird is cool?

Oh, hello, dear reader. Might I interest you in some additional seahorse facts? Several are quite weird, I assure you!

Seahorses are rather petite creatures. The largest I've had a chat with was nearly 13 inches long, whilst the smallest—a pygmy seahorse— was the size of a single grain of rice.

Even though I'm technically a fish, I don't have icky scales. I have skin—almost like you—except *mine* can change colors, so...some might say I'm *more* impressive.

Underneath my skin, my body is made of armored plates to prevent my getting crushed by evildoers. I'm practically a knight of old, like Sir Lancelot. If you wish to call me Sir Seahorse, I shan't stop you.

Our eyes can look in two directions at the same time. I believe you'd call that "talent."

Seahorse mates pair up together for life.
Each morning, after tea and shrimp, my mate and I hold tails
and perform a color-changing slow dance together. I call it

the RAINBOW TANGO.

PARTY!

I have a special bladder called a swim
bladder to help me float. It's like having a
balloon in my body, which is wonderful
because I do so enjoy party decor.

Seahorses are almost always
eating because we have no stomachs.
We suck up our food like dainty little Hoovers—
or "vacuum cleaners," as you might call them.
(Even though you'd be wrong.)

Were you so inclined, you could adopt a seahorse.
The World Animal Foundation and the World Wildlife
Fund offer such programs on their websites.

Library of Congress
Cataloging-in-Publication data
is on file with the publisher.

Text and illustrations copyright © 2020
by Cassandra Federman

First published in the United States of America
in 2020 by Albert Whitman & Company
ISBN 978-0-8075-7860-5 (hardcover)
ISBN 978-0-8075-7859-9 (ebook)
Printed in China
10 9 8 7 6 5 4 3 2 1 RRD 24 23 22 21 20

Design by Cassandra Federman

For more information about
Albert Whitman & Company, visit our
website at www.albertwhitman.com.